Nala's Magical Mitsiaq

A Story of Inuit Adoption

INHABIT
PILIRIQATIGIIT
ᐃᓄᐃᑦ ᑎᐱᕆᐊᖅᑕᐅᑎᑦ

Published by Inhabit Media Inc.
www.inhabitmedia.com

Inhabit Media Inc. (Iqaluit), P.O. Box 11125, Iqaluit, Nunavut, X0A 1H0
(Toronto), 146A Orchard View Blvd., Toronto, Ontario, M4R 1C3

Design and layout copyright © 2013 Inhabit Media Inc.
Text copyright © 2013 Jennifer Noah
Illustrations copyright © 2013 Qin Leng

Editors: Louise Flaherty, Neil Christopher, and Kelly Ward
Art Director: Ellen Ziegler

We acknowledge the support of the Canada Council for the Arts for our publishing program.

We acknowledge the support of the Department of Culture and Heritage for this publication.

Printed in Canada.

Library and Archives Canada Cataloguing in Publication

Noah, Jennifer, 1981-
    Nala's magical mitsiaq : a story of Inuit adoption / Jennifer
Noah ; [illustrated by] Qin Leng.

ISBN 978-1-927095-26-3

    I. Leng, Qin II. Title.

PS8627.O183N35 2013   jC813'.6   C2012-908630-4

Canadian Heritage   Patrimoine canadien

Nala's Magical Mitsiaq

A Story of Inuit Adoption

Jennifer Noah • Qin Leng

DEDICATIONS

To birth mothers and fathers who selflessly give life out of love. Your love gives *people* the gift of becoming *families*.

To Nuna and Qiatsuk Noah—Nakurmiik for helping the Government of Canada legally recognize the practice of Inuit custom adoption in 1960.

Ayva-Lin Qiatsuk—Thank you for choosing my belly to grow in and for making me an anaana. My first-born panik, you have taught me so much. Love you always and forever, my little Qiatsuk.

Adelle Malaika Nala—Thank you for dream-travelling to me before your birth and choosing my heart to grow in. Your journey to our family was always meant to be. Love you always and forever, my precious child.

Qiatsuk Noah
(Photo courtesy of Caroline Qiatsuk Noah)

Nala Alainga
(Photo courtesy of the Alainga family)

To Qiatsuk, your love for music and the arts has blossomed in our little Qiatsuk. The kindness and love you gave to family and community lives in the heart of your iluliq. Thank you for walking this journey with our panik in spirit.

To Nala, your legacy of lighting the way and being a strong leader shines brightly through our little Nala. Your strength and determination live on through your sauniq. Thank you for guiding our panilaaq's Earth walk in spirit.

Qiatsuk and Nala were giddy with excitement as they pulled on their pyjamas and waited for Anaana to tuck them into bed. The family planned to go sledding the next day, and the girls couldn't wait for the morning to come.

"Where do you think Ataata is going to take us sledding tomorrow?" Nala asked her sister, gleefully. "Astro Hill or Road to Nowhere?"

"Maybe he'll take us to both spots," Qiatsuk replied, matching her sister's enthusiasm. "And maybe Anaana will surprise us with hot chocolate!"

"I wonder if we will be able to see snow fairies from the top of the sledding hill," Nala squealed, as she wriggled under her covers. Qiatsuk thought about the beautiful fairies the girls often imagined dancing on the blowing snow.

"Well, I heard that snow fairies hide way up in the sky when their wings get tired." Qiatsuk giggled as she thought about it. "And they ride talking narwhals through the clouds."

"We should wear our fairy wings over our parkas tomorrow," replied Nala, matter-of-factly. "So they know that we're friendly."

The girls were taking turns imagining what the names of the snow fairies might be when their anaana walked into the bedroom and dimmed the light.

"Try to calm down and get some sleep, girls. We have a big day planned for tomorrow," Anaana reminded them gently.

Then she sat on the edge of Nala's bed, and—as she did every night—she began singing the girls their special tutaa song.

My paniit, my loves
My gifts from above
The love that binds us grows stronger each day
Making us a family in every way
Qiatsuk grew in my belly, while Nala grew in my heart
Sisters who arrived two years and two months apart
You are here with us now, and forever we will be
A loving and devoted family

With that, the sisters yawned and struggled to keep their eyes open.

"Goodnight, my loves," Anaana whispered as she kuniked their cheeks and tucked them in, knowing their dreams would be filled with wonder and magic.

The next morning, the girls jumped from their beds, bright-eyed and full of excitement for their day of sledding. They raced to the front door and got dressed in their winter gear before even thinking about having breakfast or speaking to their parents.

When she was fully zipped into her snow pants and parka, Nala finally called from the bottom of the stairs in an eager voice, "Ataata! We're ready to go see snow fairies from the top of the sledding hill! I'm going to wear my pink fairy wings so they know I'm a friend."

"Girls," Ataata replied hesitantly, "why don't you come have some breakfast and take a look out the window before you get your kamiik on?"

Nala and Qiatsuk looked at each other. They knew by the tone of Ataata's voice that the weather must have changed. It didn't look like they'd be going sledding after all. They trudged up the stairs, still in their snow gear, and stared out the window at the blizzard on the other side of the glass.

"I guess we won't be seeing any snow fairies in this whiteout," Qiatsuk whispered in a disappointed tone.

"I can't even see the neighbour's house," Nala replied.

"Well girls, you can always spend your Saturday tidying up your bedroom and doing homework," Ataata called to them teasingly from the kitchen.

The girls ate their breakfast slowly, hoping the blizzard would let up by the time they finished. They watched the white windows longingly, wishing as hard as they could that the snow would stop. After walking their breakfast dishes to the sink as slowly as possible, the girls slumped back to their seats at the table, disappointed.

"We're bored!" they whined in unison to their parents.

"Why doesn't one of you girls go get me your nasaq and we can each write down an idea for how to spend the day," Anaana suggested, brightly. "Whichever idea I pull from the nasaq first is what we'll do."

"Okay, I'll go get mine!" Nala offered with renewed excitement.

Moments later, Nala returned, and each member of the family wrote down an idea on a slip of paper and deposited it into her nasaq. Anaana shook it for a moment and finally pulled out a folded, crumpled-up piece of paper. In Nala's printing, the paper read, "Tell us what it means that Qiatsuk grew in your belly and I grew in your heart."

"Well, that's a lovely way for us to spend the morning," Anaana said, smiling. "Let's get cozy in the living room and Ataata will make us some hot chocolate."

Nala and Qiatsuk ran to the living room and cuddled up on the floor in front of the sofa. They curled up with Moon, their dog, and Rhino, their cat, as they all waited for the story to begin.

"So, you both know that Qiatsuk grew in my belly and Nala grew in my heart," Anaana began as she got comfortable on the sofa. The girls poked at their bellies and felt their hearts beating under their shirts with their hands.

"But I think what Nala is really asking is, what does that mean?"

"Yes," Nala chimed in. "I don't understand why I didn't grow in your belly like Qiatsuk did."

"Well, let me tell you both how Nala came to grow in my heart and how our family came to be."

"One night, I had a magical dream. It was wintertime, and it was very cold outside. A beautiful, smiling baby came to me. The baby didn't say anything, but our hearts seemed to know one another. I knew that this baby was meant to be a part of our family. It was like a magical mitsiaq was connecting our hearts, even though the baby was growing in a different mother's belly."

Anaana looked from Qiatsuk to Nala as she spoke. The girls listened silently, hanging on every word.

"That baby, as it turns out, was you, Nala."

"Me?" Nala exclaimed with surprise. "I came to you in a dream even before I was born?"

"Yes, Nala. After that dream I knew you were coming to our family, and I started to prepare for your arrival, even though I didn't know who your puukuluk was until much later."

"My puukuluk is Simonie!" Nala announced, proudly.

"That's right! You have always known Simonie, and you always will. She gave you life, panilaaq."

Nala thought about that for a moment.

"So I grew in your heart because of a magical mitsiaq?"

"Yes, I like to think so. My love for you as my panik is just as strong and natural as my love for Qiatsuk! Many families in Nunavut have children who grew in their anaanas' bellies and children who grew in their anaanas' hearts, just like you and Qiatsuk," Anaana explained.

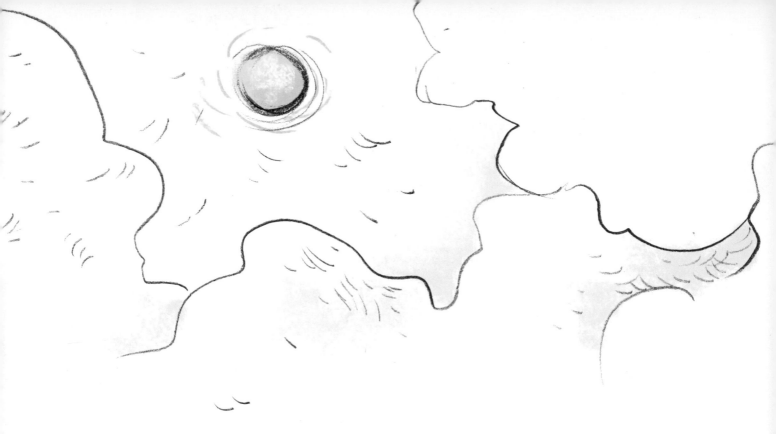

"But why do I have a puukuluk and a birth family and Qiatsuk doesn't?" Nala asked.

"Anaana and I are Qiatsuk's birth parents, Nala," Ataata explained. "Anaana gave birth to Qiatsuk, just as Simonie gave birth to you. Simonie will always be a part of you. She asked us to be your family out of love, and we welcomed you into our family with love. The way you became a part of our family is called adoption. When parents build a family by adopting a child it is called tiguarniq in Inuktitut."

"I've heard that word before, Ataata. Lots of kids in my class are adopted, but I never knew what that meant," Qiatsuk shared.

"That's right! Many Inuit kids are adopted, and adoption between Inuit families is called customary adoption or custom adoption."

"And your custom adoption was very special, Nala," Ataata beamed.

"It was?" Nala said with a grin.

"When our family and friends heard that we were hoping to adopt a baby, they shared the news with their friends, and soon the entire community had heard the news! When Simonie heard, she was very happy, and she asked us to become your anaana and ataata. After Simonie met Anaana, they got along very well, so she decided to ask Ananna to help bring you into the world!"

"When you were born," Anaana added, "Simonie asked me to cut your mitsiaq. I was so happy that your puukuluk would give me such an honour! I was invited to cut your birth mitsiaq, and all the while the magical mitsiaq that joined us together seemed to grow stronger."

Nala smiled up at her anaana.

"I was the first person to hold you, and because our hearts were already connected, we both knew we were meant to be mother and child," Anaana said.

"Do you think Simonie was sad that you and Ataata adopted me?" Nala asked.

"Of course a part of Simonie was sad. She loved you very much, Nala, and she always will. A mother's love has no beginning and no end," Anaana said, giving Nala's shoulder a loving squeeze. "It is an endless circle of love."

"And you know, girls, Aana Kitty, my anaana, was also custom adopted," Ataata added.

"She was?" the girls said in unison.

"Yes! In fact, Aana Kitty's birth and her adoption into our family helped change the laws for adoption among Inuit. Her journey made it possible for us to continue our long tradition of creating families through custom adoption."

"So Aana Kitty wasn't born with our last name?" Qiatsuk asked, surprised.

"No, she wasn't," Ataata explained, "just as Nala was born with a different name. But after Aana Kitty's parents filed some paperwork with a custom adoption officer, she became their legal panik, just as Nala became ours."

"In many custom adoptions, birth families, birth children, and adoptive families have very loving relationships that last a lifetime. That's why you spend time with Simonie and her family, and why they celebrate with us on special occasions, like your birthday," Anaana said.

"And guess what?" Ataata said with a smile. "Ningiuq, Simonie's mother, is my cousin through Aana Kitty's birth family. So you see, panilaaq, we are all connected!"

"So, I grew in Anaana's heart, I have our family's last name, and you are my anaana and ataata," Nala affirmed.

"Yes, exactly," Anaana replied, happily.

"But I've always noticed that I don't really look like my angiju. Does that mean we're not *real* sisters?"

"Nala, you and Qiatsuk are sisters in every sense of the word! You belong to the same family, and you love each other. All you really need to be a family is love, my child, and that is something we have a whole lot of!" Anaana exclaimed.

"And I know you're my real sister because you're my best friend and we like all the same things," Qiatsuk added.

"Yeah! And we must be real sisters if all you need to be a family is love, because I love Qiatsuk the most out of anybody in the whole wide world!" exclaimed Nala.

Qiatsuk kuniked her nukaq and gave her a hug.

"Did you know, panilaaq, that your new birth certificate arrived on your very first Christmas Eve? You finally had our family name and were officially our panik! It was the best Christmas gift we ever could have asked for!" recounted Ataata.

"Wow, I didn't know that the story of how I came to be part of our family was so special. I'm so happy that my magical mitsiaq chose your hearts so that you could be my parents. And I'm so happy that I get to have the best angiju in the world!" said Nala with a grin. "And I'm also thankful to our great-grandparents for adopting Aana Kitty so that I could be adopted by you!"

"We are very happy that your magical mitsiaq chose us to be your parents, too, our dear, sweet Nala. We love you very much," Anaana shared with a loving smile.

"Hey, look!" Qiatsuk exclaimed. "The blizzard has let up! I can see Inuksuk High School and the neighbours' houses through the window! Can we still have our day of sledding?" Qiatsuk and Nala looked expectantly at their parents.

"Of course we can!" Ataata exclaimed.

And with that, the sisters squealed with excitement and ran to pull their parkas and kamiik back on.

The whole family enjoyed the rest of the afternoon outside, looking for snow fairies from the top of the best sledding hill in Iqaluit.

GLOSSARY OF INUKTITUT TERMS

aana	grandmother, father's mother, South Baffin dialect
anaana	mother
angiju	older sibling, same gender
ataata	father
iluliq	great-grandchild, Baffin Dialect
kamiik	waterproof boots made from sealskin or caribou skin
kunik	an Inuit kiss; breathing in the skin and creating suction with the nose to show affection
mitsiaq	umbilical cord
nakurmiik	thank you, South Baffin dialect
nasaq	hat
ningiuq	grandmother, mother's mother, North Baffin dialect
nukaq	younger sibling, same gender
panik	daughter
panilaaq	youngest/smallest daughter
puukuluk	birth mother
sauniq	one's namesake
tiguarniq	the act of adopting
tutaa	term for bedtime/sleep used with very young children

EPILOGUE

Nala's Magical Mitsiaq was written because I wanted to be able to read a children's story to my panik to which she could relate. My daughter Adelle has an adoption story *and* a birth story. Her journey to find us was quite remarkable, but our story is also commonplace among Inuit, and within Nunavut, as many other families have been created through adoption. I also wrote this story so that children who have been adopted from Nunavut to other parts of Canada will know how amazing the journey they took to find their families was, and to show those children how revered and celebrated the practice of adoption is among Inuit.

Adoption can look different for every family. Whether the adoption is international or domestic, whether the adoption is open or closed, or whether a child is adopted as a baby or later in life, at the heart of adoption is love.

Inuit custom adoption empowers both the birth family and adopting family to discuss openly what the adoption will look like, including ongoing roles the birth family may have with the child and the importance of namesakes and choosing names for the child. Inuit custom adoption is recognized by the Government of Canada as a respected traditional practice, in which birth families choose adoptive families for their children. At least one of the adopting parents in a custom adoption must to be of Inuit descent. The practice of adoption among Inuit is a time-honoured custom that celebrates building families through love. I hope *Nala's Magical Mitsiaq* will bring those who read it a deeper understanding of what adoption means, and most of all, that it will help children of adoption to know how much they are loved!

Below are some words of wisdom about Inuit custom adoption from women who have experienced this special Inuit tradition.

. . My mom gave up two of my siblings because they [the adoptive family] couldn't have babies. To help that family grow, she gave them children out of love. I didn't even know my sister had been adopted out because she was at our house all of the time. Before these days, there was no need to have closed boundaries between birth and adopting families, we were just all family." —Mary

"I said I would never adopt. Then my daughter got pregnant and wanted to continue with her school and said, 'Mom, do you want to adopt my baby?' It was a boy. We didn't have our own son. We adopted him. He's going to be eleven next month. I used to think that I would never adopt, but when you adopt . . . it is more loving. There is more love toward that adoptee . . . Sometimes my son calls me grandmother, but mostly [he calls me] Anaana, and [he calls] his birth mother, my daughter, Mom. There is a special love for a child that you adopt; it is very strong." —Eena

"My adopted baby brother changed my life. Before I adopted my daughter, I dreamed and hoped to be able to adopt a little girl. I was with her [my daughter's birth mother] in her labour. It seems like since that day my life changed. It was so exciting. I couldn't stop smiling. I was so happy. I just kept smiling to myself." —Jeannie

"I have adopted eight children . . . This practice is very good for Inuit because it really helps your body and soul and the bonds [between parents and children]. When you adopt—if you're willing to adopt—it works. It's an important tradition for Inuit. It was a totally different bond whenever we adopted each child. The bonds between us and the families we adopted from are strong. They always appreciated us raising their babies or their grandkids. It was very different with each of the eight families [that we adopted from]. I never looked for babies. They always came to us and asked us to adopt. Part of survival was to adopt, but mostly [we adopted] out of love." —Taina

"We are all adopted. My mother is not my natural mother, but she adopted me from her brother. My biological parents let my mother adopt me. The bond [I have] is very strong for my parents; that is how I feel. My parents loved all of us like we were their own biological children. I am the oldest one. Love is the strongest point in life, and the most encouraging."—Susie

"Back then, when Inuit were still living in iglus, there was a couple who were supposed to adopt a baby who didn't actually get to keep that baby. The couple came back to their iglu, crying after going to try to adopt their baby. Through love, my parents gave them a son when they saw them hurting. Through love, Inuit would give a baby. That is Inuit traditional knowledge, to pass that love to another family if they cannot have a baby. Through love, Inuit give a human being to another human being."—Eena

Left-Right: Susie Eetuk, Eena Kanayuk, Jeannie Smith, Mary Akpalialuk, Taina Nuyalia

Jennifer Noah is a first-time author who grew up in the South but always had a fondness for the North. She would often write short stories about Inuit children in her primary school years. Jennifer moved to Iqaluit in her mid-twenties, where she continued her work in the field of mental health and addictions counselling. She later transitioned into a youth health researcher role, where she worked collaboratively with communities to develop an evidence-based model for youth wellness and empowerment programs in Nunavut that reflect Nunavummiut voices, Inuit Qaujimajatuqangit, and Inuit values. Through her work, she was privileged to hear stories and wisdom from many Nunavummiut. She enjoys watching youth discovering a deeper understanding of Inuit culture and traditions as they listen to the stories and wisdom of their elders. Jennifer and her husband have two children, one of whom was traditionally custom adopted through family. She delights in spending time with her daughters as she watches them learn and grow. Jennifer hopes to continue writing for children and sharing the rich knowledge and traditions of Inuit through her written work.

Qin Leng was born in Shanghai and lived in France and Montreal. She now lives and works as a designer and illustrator in Toronto. Her father, an artist himself, was a great influence on her. She grew up surrounded by paintings, and it became second nature for her to express herself through art. She graduated from The Mel Hoppenheim School of Cinema and has received many awards for her animated short films and artwork. Qin Leng always loved to illustrate the innocence of children and has developed a passion for children's books. She has published numerous picture books in Canada, the United States, and South Korea.